For Eriko Arikawa McGee and our Japanese family –
especially Mitsuyuki, Kazuko and Mitsuko ~ M M

For my sister Susan R Macnaughton ~ T M

Copyright © 2006 by Good Books, Intercourse, PA 17534
International Standard Book Number: 1-56148-513-6
Library of Congress Catalog Card Number: 2005021221

Text copyright © Marni McGee 2006
Illustrations copyright © Tina Macnaughton 2006

Original edition published in English by Little Tiger Press,
an imprint of Magi Publications, London, England, 2006.

Printed in China

Library of Congress Cataloging-in-Publication Data

McGee, Marni.
While angels watch / Marni McGee and pictures by Tina Macnaughton.
p. cm.

Summary: Animals recall how angels were involved in the creation of the Earth,
and confide that they are still here teaching birds how to sing and fly, helping
the lost find their way, and guarding and guiding children each day and night.
ISBN 1-56148-513-6 (hardcover : alk. paper) [1. Angels--Fiction. 2. Animals--Fiction.
3. Stories in rhyme.] I. Macnaughton, Tina, ill. II. Title.
PZ8.3.M1564Whi 2006
[E]--dc22

2005021221

While Angels Watch

Marni McGee   Tina Macnaughton

Good Books

Intercourse, PA 17534
800/762-7171
www.GoodBks.com

Long ago, when the world was new,
The Angels all had work to do.
They picked the colors of the dawn,
Clouds of pink and skies of blue.

Some taught dolphins how to swim,
To dance in sparkling seas . . .
Diving down with silvery fish,
Then leaping up with playful ease.

Some showed spiders how to spin
And helped them hang their webs in trees.
The smallest Angels of them all
Painted stripes on bumblebees.

Other Angels told the roosters
Where to perch and when to crow.
But where did all those Angels go?
Where are they now? Does no one know?

"I've heard," said Lamb, "that once they came
To sing a newborn baby's birth.
The hillside glowed with Angels' light.
I wonder, are they still on Earth?"

"The Angels are still here," said Owl.
"They teach our babies how to sing.
They show us how to nest and fly,
To sail the sky on silent wing."

"Once," said Calf, "I wandered off –
Far from mother, far from hay.
I could not find my cozy barn
Until an Angel showed the way."

"I heard Angels," murmured Dog,
"On the day my pups were born.
As each one raised its tiny head,
A joyful Angel blew her horn."

"I've seen Angels play," said Hare.
"They race with Fox and dark-eyed Deer.
And when a whispering river speaks,
Angels gather close to hear."

"But what of children?" wondered Duck.
"They have no feathers, have no fur.
Could Angels care for *them* as well?
They cannot fly nor even purr!"

"The Angels love each one," said Cat.
"I've watched and know it's true.
Angels hover round by day
To guide in all that children do."

"And I have seen with my green eyes:
At night the Angels guard their beds.
The children sleep with happy dreams
When gentle Angels touch their heads."